Emmy
the Exaggerating
Elephant

Fenton
the Fearful Frog

Gertie
the Grungy Goat

H
the Happy
Hamster

Ivy
the Impatient
Iguana

Ollie
the Obedient
Ostrich

Perry
the Polite
Porcupine

Queenie
the Quiet Quail

Rupert
the Resourceful
Rhinoceros

Wendy
the Wise
Woodchuck

Xavier
the X-ploring
Xenops

Yori
the Yucky Yak

Ziggy
the Zippy Zebra

NOTE TO PARENTS

<u>Nelly, That's Not Nice!</u>
A story about trust

In this story, Nelly the Naughty Newt is habitually less than honest. Like the boy who cried "wolf," Nelly finds out that because people have learned not to trust her, they accuse her of wrongdoing even when she's blameless.

In addition to enjoying this exciting story with your child, you can use it to teach a gentle lesson about the character-building value of trustworthiness. Explain how important it is to be reliable and to do the right thing, such as respecting other people's property.

You can also use this story to introduce the letter **N**. As you read about Nelly the Naughty Newt, ask your child to listen for all the **N** words and to point to the objects that begin with **N**. When you've finished reading the story, your child will enjoy doing the activity at the end of the book.

The AlphaPets™ characters were conceived and created by Ruth Lerner Perle.
Characters interpreted and designed by Deborah Colvin Borgo.
Cover/book design and production by Norton & Company.
Logo design by Deborah Colvin Borgo and Nancy S. Norton.
Edited by Ruth Lerner Perle.
Printed and Manufactured in the United States of America

Nelly,
That's Not Nice!

SHIRLEY BOGART

Illustrated by Richard Max Kolding

Grolier Enterprises Inc.,   Danbury, Connecticut

One nice day, Nelly the Naughty Newt went to play in the park. She saw some of her AlphaPet friends jumping rope, tossing Frisbees, and playing with their new yo-yos.

Nelly took her yo-yo out of her pocket and ran over to where the others were playing.

"Hi, Nelly," said Sylvester the Stubborn Squirrel. "Watch my trick." Sylvester swung his yo-yo up in the air and made it come down again behind his back.

"That's okay," Nelly said, "but watch this." She tossed her yo-yo up in the air and was about to pull it back, when *pop*, the string broke. Nelly's yo-yo fell to the ground.

"My yo-yo!" cried Nelly. "Now what will I play with?"

Jingle jingle! Just then, the ice-cream wagon came driving by. "We'll try to fix your yo-yo later," said Herbie the Happy Hamster. "Let's get some ice cream!" He took Sylvester by the hand and they ran off.

Fenton the Fearful Frog put his yo-yo carefully into his bag and followed Herbie. "I hope the ice cream won't be too cold, or drip on my new shirt," Fenton said.

As soon as everybody was gone, Nelly looked around. No one was watching her. She took Fenton's yo-yo out of his bag and put her broken one in its place.

"Now I have a yo-yo that works," Nelly thought. "I'm sure Fenton can fix the broken one."

Suddenly Nelly heard a voice.

"Nelly, that's not nice!" called the voice. "Would you like it if someone took *your* yo-yo?"

Nelly looked up. There was Xavier the X-ploring Xenops, reaching for his Frisbee.

"You took Fenton's yo-yo," Xavier said. "If you want a yo-yo that works, you should fix the old one, or buy a new one."

Nelly felt her face grow hot, and she hung her head. "I didn't think Fenton would mind," she said.

"Well, it's wrong to take things that don't belong to you," Xavier said. "Just think how you would feel if someone took something of yours."

Nelly put the yo-yo back in Fenton's bag and started for home. On her way, she passed Albert the Absent-minded Alligator's house. There was a neatly folded newspaper lying on his front steps.

"Oh, goody!" Nelly thought. "I want to know what time the Cake Sale starts tomorrow. Maybe there's an article about it in the paper."

Nelly sat down on Albert's front steps and unfolded his newspaper.

She turned the pages looking for the Cake Sale announcement. The first page had world news. "No, I don't want world news," Nelly said, and she threw the page on the lawn.

The next page had advertising notices. "No, I'm not interested in the ads," Nelly said. She pushed that page aside. She turned page after page. Then, next to the comics, Nelly noticed instructions for making a Nifty Nautical Newspaper Hat.

"Oh, goody," she said. "I'll make a sailor hat!"

Nelly took one page of the newspaper and started to fold it.

Just then Albert came to the door. "Look what you've done to my paper! Now I won't be able to read it!" he cried. "Nelly, that's not nice!"

"I just wanted to know when the Cake Sale starts," said Nelly. "I'm going with Wendy, and we want to be the first ones there."

"Never mind, Nelly. If you want to borrow something, you should ask first. And if you do borrow it, you should return it the way you found it," said Albert.

Nelly helped Albert pick up the papers, and then she ran home.

The next day, when Nelly and Wendy the Wise Woodchuck arrived at the Cake Sale, there was already a long line of AlphaPets waiting their turn to get in.

"Let's not stand in this old line," Nelly whispered to Wendy. "I know how we can sneak in the back door."

"No, no, Nelly, that's not nice!" Wendy said. "You wouldn't like it if *you* waited and someone got in ahead of you!"

"But nobody will know!" Nelly said.

"Nobody *has* to know," Wendy answered. "If I do something wrong, *I* know, and that's bad enough."

BAKE SALE
TODAY
BUY A RAFFLE TICKET
WIN A NECKLACE

When it was finally their turn, Wendy and Nelly bought their tickets and walked into the big gym. There were tables of cakes, pies, brownies, doughnuts, and cookies all laid out on colorful napkins.

Wendy and Nelly passed a long table. On it were the cakes that had won prizes in the Cake Bake Contest.

Near the cakes, they saw a beautiful purple and green necklace on display.

"That's the prize necklace that's being raffled off!" said Ziggy the Zippy Zebra.

"I'd love to have a necklace like that!" Nelly said.

"Let's buy some raffle tickets," Wendy suggested. "Maybe one of us will have the lucky winning number."

Nelly and Wendy took nickels out of their pockets and they each bought a raffle ticket. Nelly's number was 19. Wendy's number was 99.

Just then, Rupert the Resourceful Rhinoceros walked by eating a doughnut all covered with chocolate.

"Ooh, that looks delicious," said Nelly.

"It is," said Rupert. "Want a bite?"

"Oh, yes!" Nelly said. She took one little bite. Then she took another *big* bite, and finished the whole doughnut!

"Hey, Nelly, that's not nice!" shouted Rupert. "You're supposed to leave some for me. I offered you a *bite*, not the whole doughnut."

"Oops! Sorry, Rupert," Nelly said, and she ran off.

Soon it was time for the raffle. Ziggy called everyone to attention.

"Ladies and Gentlemen," he said. "It's time to pick the winning raffle ticket. As you all know, the winner will receive this beautiful necklace."

Ziggy pointed to where the necklace was displayed. Everyone looked to where he was pointing, but there was no necklace! All they could see were two big nails. The necklace was gone!

"Where is the necklace?" cried Delilah the Demanding Duck. "We must find it!"

The AlphaPets looked everywhere. They looked under the tables. No necklace. They looked behind the chairs. No necklace. They looked all over the floor and beneath the carpets, but the necklace was nowhere to be found.

"Why waste any more time looking?" someone shouted. "I'll bet Nelly took it!"

"That's right!" cried someone else. "She always takes things that don't belong to her."

"Oh, no!" Nelly cried. "I didn't take the necklace!"

"And she doesn't always tell the truth, either," somebody else yelled.

"Come on, Nelly," Sylvester said. "You'd better return the necklace."

"But I really *didn't* take it!" Nelly said.

"Well, you took my yo-yo!" said Fenton.

"And my newspaper!" shouted Albert.

"And my doughnut!" Rupert added.

Sylvester pointed to Nelly's pocket. "What's that in your pocket? Could it be the necklace, by any chance?" he asked.

Nelly burst into tears. She reached into her pocket and pulled out her handkerchief to show everyone. "See, this is all I have in my pocket," she said.

Suddenly Ollie the Obedient Ostrich came running over.
He was holding his prize-winning cake.

"Hey, everybody! Look at this!" he shouted.

Ollie's cake had purple flowers and green swirls on
it. But there was something else decorating the top—
something Ollie had not put there.

"It's the necklace!" cried Ziggy. "It must have fallen off
and landed on top of the cake. It looks just like Ollie's
decorations. That's why nobody noticed."

"I think we owe somebody an apology," Wendy said. "We're all sorry that we accused you of taking the necklace, Nelly." Everyone agreed.

"That's the truth," added Tina the Truthful Tiger. "And it's also true that people who do naughty things are the first ones to be blamed, even when it's not their fault."

"I guess so," Nelly said. "I'll try to change my ways, I promise. From now on you'll see a nice, new Nelly—a Nelly you can trust!"

"Time for the raffle!" Ziggy shouted. He reached into the bowl and picked the winning ticket. It was number 19.

Nelly held up her ticket. "That's my number! I won! I won!" she yelled.

Nelly was so happy, and all the AlphaPets were happy for her, too.

From then on, Nelly tried her best to be nice.

When Nelly's balloon broke,
she didn't take Herbie's.
She bought another one.

When she saw Albert's new
scooter, she didn't just take it.
Nelly asked if she could ride it.

When she went to the movies
with Perry the Polite Porcupine,
she waited patiently in line
to buy a ticket.

And when Gertie the Grungy Goat
offered her some pretzels,
Nelly didn't eat them all up.
She took a few from the bag
and gave the rest back to Gertie.

Nelly tried hard to do her best. All the AlphaPets were
proud of Nelly—the new Nelly they could trust.

Remember these nifty words with me.

nest

nickel

needle

nail

newspaper

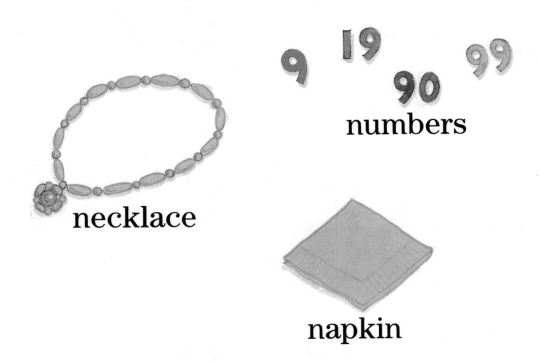

necklace

numbers

napkin

Look back at the pictures in this book and find these and other things that start with N.

Know Your Alphabet

Aa Bb

Gg Hh

Mm Nn Oo Pp

Uu Vv Ww